"Mercy, it's the revolution and I'm in my bathrobe."

"Mercy, it's the revolution and I'm in my bathrobe."

More Sylvia by Nicole Hollander

St. Martin's Press, New York

For information, write: St. Martin's Press,
175 Fifth Avenue, New York, N.Y. 10010
Manufactured in the United States of America

Design by Tom Greenfelder and Nicole Hollander
10 9 8 7 6 5 4 3 2 1
First Edition

"College Reunion Fantasy No. 1 and 2" first appeared in *Ms.* Magazine.

Library of Congress Cataloging in Publication Data

Hollander, Nicole.
    "Mercy, it's the revolution and I'm in my bathrobe".

    1. American wit and humor, Pictorial.   I. Title.
NC1429.H588A4   1982   741.5'973   81-18216
ISBN 0-312-53013-7 (pbk.)   AACR2

8

9

10

11

12

13

14

15

16

17

MEDICAL NEWS

DOCTORS RECOGNIZE WOMEN'S SUFFRAGE

BALTIMORE (AP) The American Medical Association announced today that women do have menstrual cramps.

"Yeah, we thought it was all in their heads, but its not. We still don't wanna talk about it though," said an association spokesman.

19

20

21

22

23

24

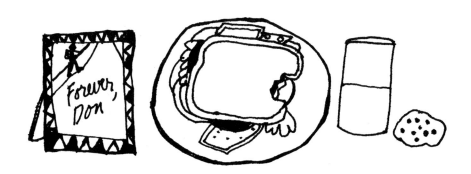

26

27

SEX QUESTIONNAIRE

ARE YOU NORMAL?

T. ☐ **F.** ☐ 1. YOU FEEL TENSE WHEN YOU READ A SURVEY OF SEXUAL PREFERENCES AND PRACTICES UNTIL YOU FIND OUT THAT OTHER PEOPLE DO WHAT YOU DO OR FANTASIZE ABOUT DOING WHAT YOU DO.

T. ☐ **F.** ☐ 2. YOU NEVER FIND YOUR PARTICULAR PREFERENCE IN A SURVEY OF SEXUAL PREFERENCES AND PRACTICES.

29

30

31

32

33

34

35

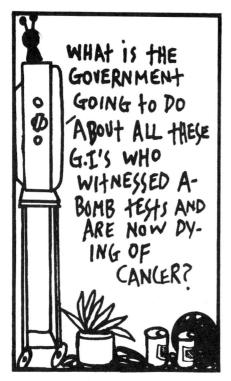

WHAT IS THE GOVERNMENT GOING TO DO ABOUT ALL THESE G.I.'S WHO WITNESSED A-BOMB TESTS AND ARE NOW DYING OF CANCER?

THE GOVERNMENT GETS BLAMED FOR EVERYTHING. SOME VIETNAM VET SLIPS

ON A BANANA PEEL, RIGHT AWAY HE BLAMES IT ON AGENT ORANGE.

37

38

SYLVIA STANDS UP

39

40

41

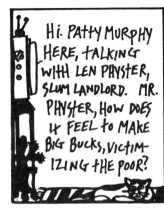

42

43

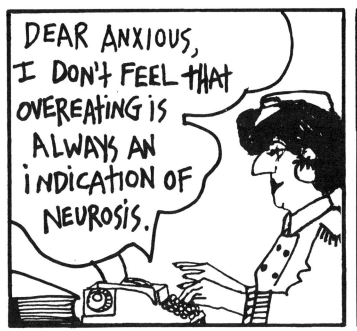

44

45

46

47

FANTASIES

WOMEN WILL SHAKE OFF THE INFLUENCE OF GODLESS COMMUNISM AND RETURN TO THEIR FIRST DUTY AS WIVES AND MOTHERS EARLY NEXT YEAR.

49

50

53

54

55

56

57

58

59

THE PUBLISHER OF THE NATIONAL ENQUIRER CANDIDLY REVEALED TODAY...

THAT EVERYTHING THEY WRITE ABOUT MOVIE STARS IS "PURE BULL,"

BUT ALL THE STUFF ABOUT U.F.O.'s IS TRUE.

PATTY MURPHY NEWS

DEAR MEG, I...

DEAR MEG, THEY...

DEAR MEG, MORE ABOUT THAT LATER. HOW ARE SAM AND THE BOYS?

TATTOO PROBLEMS

61

63

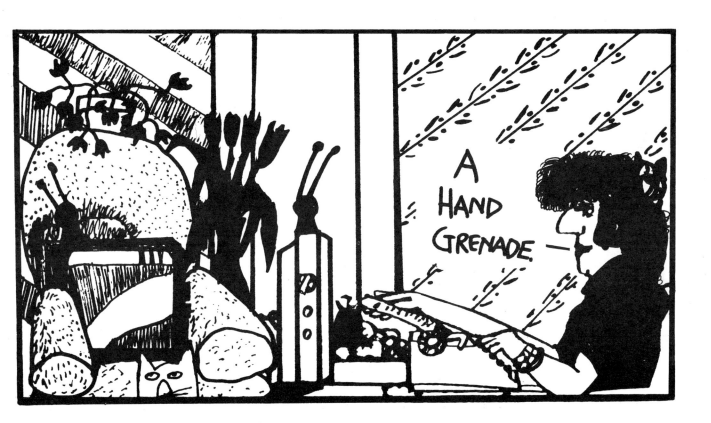

65

67

68

71

72,

ANIMAL FANTASIES

75

76

80

82

83

DO PEOPLE LEAVE THE ROOM WHEN YOU TELL YOUR STORY ABOUT HOW YOU WERE ALMOST ARRESTED...

DURING A PEACE MARCH? TELL ME YOUR MOST BORING PERSONAL ANECDOTE, AND I WILL GIVE IT MY UNDIVIDED ATTENTION. SYLVIA'S SPECIAL SERVICES, $25 FOR HALF AN HOUR. GROUP LISTENING AVAILABLE. SHARP INTAKES OF BREATH, EXTRA.

NOBODY DOES AN HONEST DAY'S WORK ANYMORE—THEY ALL WANT SOMETHING FOR NOTHING.

YOU'RE SO RIGHT— YOU HIT THE NAIL RIGHT ON THE HEAD.

AND KIDS TODAY, ALL THEY WANT IS TO DRINK AND SMOKE DOPE. I WOULDN'T GIVE YOU A NICKEL FOR THE LOT.

IT'S SO TRUE RIGHT, THEY HAVE IT TOO EASY.

IF THEY CAN'T SPEAK THE LANGUAGE SEND 'EM BACK

YOU'RE SO RIGHT, SO RIGHT.

TIME'S UP.

85

TONIGHT A CHICAGO WOMAN WAS ARRESTED FOR ALLEGEDLY RUBBING PORCELANA FADE CREAM...

ALL OVER HER HUSBAND WHILE HE WAS TAKING A NAP.

NEXT: NEWS IN BRIEF.

ANNETTE FUNICELLO TELLS ALL.

I'M GETTING SO FAT, I CAN'T ZIP UP MY SKIRTS.

IT'S NOT YOU; IT'S THE GARMENT MANUFACTURERS.

THEY'VE BEEN MAKING CLOTHES SMALLER, TO SAVE ON MATERIAL.

I'M ACTUALLY A SIZE 9, BUT I'M FORCED TO WEAR A SIZE 14.

87

FANTASIES

YOUR FIGURE WILL BE IN FASHION NEXT YEAR.

89

HANGAR 18: THE MOVIE THAT BLOWS THE LID OFF OUR NATION'S MOST CAREFULLY GUARDED MILITARY SECRET!

THE MOVIE THAT ANSWERS THE QUESTION: "DID THE U.S. GOVERNMENT GET THE SOPHISTICATED TECHNOLOGY FOR

91

93

94

95

96

97

COLLEGE REUNION FANTASY NO. 1

PICTURES OF → HUSBAND, CHILDREN, SUMMERHOUSE.

SLIM HIPS

BRIEFCASE/ PORTFOLIO

ME

EXPENSIVE SHOES

EVERYONE ELSE

99

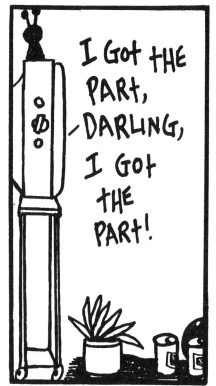

101

102

103

...It picks up each woman's special chemistry.

Cachet, the perfume no two women can wear.

More than two

And they have to evacuate the area.

105

THIS IS PATTY MURPHY, TALKING WITH DR. ETTA BRADLEY, PSYCHOLOGIST AND PROFESSIONAL NEWSPAPER READER.

DR. BRADLEY, WHY DID YOU BECOME A P.N.R.?

PATTY, I'VE TREATED MANY PEOPLE WHO WERE SO DEPRESSED AFTER READING THEIR MORNING NEWSPAPER THAT THEY COULDN'T LEAVE THE HOUSE.

ONCE I STARTED READING THE NEWSPAPER FOR THEM, THEY WERE ABLE TO LEAD NORMAL LIVES. SOME EVEN GOT JOBS.

DR. BRADLEY, CAN YOU GIVE US AN EXAMPLE OF THE KIND OF SERVICE YOU OFFER YOUR CLIENTS?

WELL PATTY, SAY I READ IN THE PAPER THAT FOOD PRICES HAVE SKYROCKETED... I'D CALL MRS. JONES AND SAY: "HI, ETHEL, IF YOU'RE GOING SHOPPING TODAY,

BRING 2½ TIMES THE MONEY YOU BROUGHT IN 1967."

LATE TODAY: 7 WOMEN TOOK CONTROL OF A DOWNTOWN GYNECOLOGIST'S OFFICE.

NEWS BREAK WITH PATTY

CALLING THEMSELVES "THE FEBRUARY 5TH MOVEMENT," THE WOMEN SAID:

"WE JUST GOT FED UP WAITING FOR HIM!" FILM AT 11:00.

OH DARLING, A CUISINART! FOR ME? OH, HOW DID YOU KNOW?

A CUISINART! FOR ME! OH, I HAD MY FINGERS CROSSED. I WANTED THIS MORE THAN ANYTHING...

MORE THAN LEOPARD-SKIN BIKINI PANTS, OR ANYTHING.

YOU BELIEVE THAT, I'VE GOT SOME LAND I'D LIKE TO SHOW YOU.

COLLEGE REUNION FANTASY NO. 2

PICTURES OF → HUSBAND, CHILDREN, SUMMERHOUSE.

SLIM HIPS

BRIEFCASE/PORTFOLIO

EVERYONE ELSE

EXPENSIVE SHOES

ME

109

111

112

113

Hi! Patty Murphy here in Washington, where the Supreme Court

Has just ruled that busing to achieve integration is unconstitutional.

"If they want it", said one Justice, "Let them use Car Pools!"

love from all of us.

115

116

MEDICAL NEWS

 RESEARCHERS IN AUSTRALIA SAY THAT IT WILL SOON BE POSSIBLE FOR MEN TO BEAR CHILDREN.

 AN EMBRYO FERTILIZED IN A LAB COULD BE IMPLANTED AND WE COULD DELIVER BY CESAREAN SECTION.

 NATURALLY AS SOON AS MEN BECOME INVOLVED IN THE PREGNANCY BUSINESS, WE WILL MAKE IT MORE EFFICIENT.

 WE CAN PROBABLY DO THE WHOLE DEAL IN 5 OR 6 MONTHS.

THIS COMMERCIAL IS FOR ALL THOSE WOMEN, OVER 30, OUT THERE WHO HOPED TO GET THROUGH AN EVENING OF TELEVISION WITHOUT SEEING AN AD FOR A MOISTURIZER...

THAT WOULD SEND A THRILL OF FEAR AND INADEQUACY COURSING THROUGH THEIR LOWER ABDOMEN,

WHICH PANG CAN ONLY BE ASSUAGED BY BUYING A VASTLY OVER-PRICED PREPARATION OF MINERAL OIL AND WATER.

OR, BY PUTTING YOUR FOOT THROUGH THE SET.

DEAR FRAZZLED,

NETWORKING AND DRESSING FOR SUCCESS ARE NOT ENDS IN THEMSELVES.

SOON YOU SHOULD START LOOKING FOR A JOB.

119

120

122

123

124

125

127